STUPID BABY

This edition first published in 2012 by Gecko Press
PO Box 9335, Marion Square, Wellington 6141, New Zealand
info@geckopress.com

Distributed in the UK by Bounce Sales & Marketing

English language edition © Gecko Press Ltd 2012

Original title: Bébé Cadum
Text and illustrations by Stephanie Blake
© 2006, l'école des loisirs, Paris

A catalogue record for this book is available from the National Library of New Zealand.

Translated by Linda Burgess
Edited by Penelope Todd
Typeset by Luke Kelly, New Zealand
Printed by Everbest, China

ISBN hardback: 978-1-877579-31-8
ISBN paperback: 978-1-877579-32-5

For more curiously good books, visit www.geckopress.com

Stephanie Blake

Stupid Baby

GECKO PRESS

Simon
has built a
very,
very,
very
tall
rocket.

Ka-boom!

goes
the
rocket.

"Shhhhhh!"

says Simon's mother.

"You must play
very quietly.
We have a tiny,
tiny
little baby
in the house."

Simon peeks into
the baby's bedroom.

"Go back where you
came from,

stupid baby."

**Suddenly,
Simon starts to worry
about all sorts of things.**

"When's that stupid baby going back to the hospital?" asks Simon.

"But Simon, he's your little brother. You know perfectly well he's here to stay."

"Forever?"

"Forever,
my little rabbit."

"Goodnight, my little rabbit,"
says his mother.
"Goodnight, my little rabbit,"
says his father.

"Goodnight," says Simon.
"Mummy, you haven't kissed me."

"Yes, I have."

"Hug me again," begs Simon.
So his mother hugs him again,
and his father does too.

But Simon can't sleep.
He lies awake for hours and hours ...

He finds himself thinking of a wolf.
A
big
bad
wolf.

He thinks about all kinds of wolves.
Father wolves and mother wolves.
Sister wolves and brother wolves.
Even baby wolves.

All of a sudden,
Simon knows
there are thousands of wolves
right outside.

A thousand-million

big
bad
wolves

who are going to eat him

Simon runs to his parents.
He stands there, not making a sound.

"Go back to bed, my little rabbit,"
says his father.

"I can't. There are wolves in my room.
Can I come in with you?"

"ABSOLUTELY NOT!"

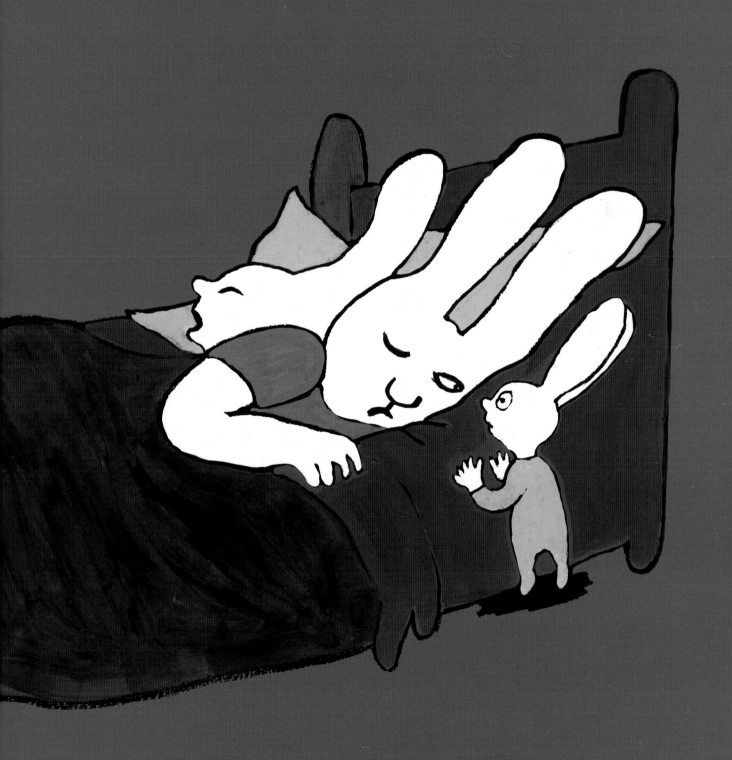

In the hall,
Simon can hear
funny noises.

Babbling
and
gabbling,

burbling
and
gurgling.

"Stupid baby!"
says Simon.

"Blabba-gabba-poo-poo Burble-gurgle-bum!"

Simon's little brother replies.

"Come with me,
my stupid little baby!
You can't stay here.
The

big

bad

wolves

are everywhere.
Come on,
I'll look after you,
my tiny,

tiny

stupid little baby."

**And that's
exactly
what
he
does.**